E   SAUNDERS, Susan *Cop. 1*
SAU

A sniff in time

A
Sniff in Time

by SUSAN SAUNDERS

with pictures by MICHAEL MARIANO

Atheneum   New York   1982

Library of Congress Cataloging in Publication Data

Saunders, Susan.   A Sniff in time.

   Summary: One day in James' life is much like the next
until a hungry wizard drops by for dinner and leaves
James with the unsettling ability to smell into the future.
   [1. Smell—Fiction. 2. Magic—Fiction] I. Mariano,
Michael, ill. II. Title.
PZ7.S2577Sn   [E]   81-10763
ISBN: 0-689-30890-6   AACR2

Published simultaneously in Canada by McClelland & Stewart, LTD.
Composition by Dix Typographers, Syracuse, New York
Printed and bound by Halliday Lithographers,
West Hanover, Massachusetts
Calligraphic title on title page by Anita Karl
First Edition

For Gillian Smith

James was a farmer,

like his father before him,

and his grandfather before that.

He milked the cows,

he plowed the fields.

He planted and tended

and harvested the crops.

At night he slept in a very old house

that he shared with his widowed mother.

One day followed another:

each year was much like the next.

"Life holds no surprises for me,"

James often said, somewhat sadly.

T hen one evening, late,

after his mother had gone to bed,

James heard a knock at the door.

"I'm the wizard Razzmatazz,"

said the stranger outside,

"traveling incognito.

For a good meal

I'll look into your future."

He covered his eyes with his hands.

"I see a boat. You will spend

the rest of your life on a boat."

"A boat? I've never even seen the ocean," said James.

"And all there is to eat at this time of year is turnips."

8 "Some soup?" asked Razzmatazz.

"For a hot bowl of soup,

I'll let you see into the future for yourself."

"Only turnips," said James.

"What about bread?" said Razzmatazz. "With butter?

For that I'll let you hear into the future."

"All I have is turnips," said James.

"Besides, I don't believe you are a wizard."

"Not a wizard!" snapped Razzmatazz.

He ate all the turnips in the pot

and what was left on James' plate as well.

"*Smell* into the future is all that deserves."

"Smell into the future?" said James.

Razzmatazz waved his left hand in front of James' nose

and sneezed three times, loudly.

"It's yours," he said, "forever."

He slammed the door closed behind him.

"How does it work?" James called through the window.

But Razzmatazz was gone.

10

James sat down and waited.

And waited.

When nothing happened,

he forgot about the stranger

and went to bed.

The next morning

just after he woke up,

James sneezed three times, loudly.

With his next breath,

his head was filled with the scent of apple blossoms

and clover and brand-new grass.

"Spring!" James said to himself.

"It's time to plant."

He went straight to the barn

and hitched the horse to the plow.

"James," his mother said
when she found him in the field,
"what are you doing?"

"Planting," James answered.
"It's spring. Can't you smell it?"

14

"Go right home and get into bed.
You must be feverish," James' mother said.
"There's still ice on the ground."
And so there was.

James drove the horse back to the barn,
feeling a little silly.
But he didn't think of the stranger.
Not yet.

The winter soon passed,
and spring came.

One warm day

after James milked the cows,

he opened the barn door

to let them graze on the tender spring grass.

But before he could get on with his chores

he sneezed three times, loudly.

He took a deep breath . . .

the air smelled sharp and wet,

the way it does before a storm breaks.

17

James hurried after the cows

and locked them into the barn again.

The cows spent the day,

which was sunny and clear,

kicking down their stalls.

By the evening they were so angry

they wouldn't give any milk.

And James' mother had no cream

for her tea.

"But, James," she said,

"the sky was as blue as could be."

James just shook his head—

he still hadn't remembered the stranger.

That night, in the midst of a dream,

James sneezed three times, loudly.

He sat straight up in bed

and took a deep breath.

Smoke! It tickled his nose

and caught at his throat.

"Fire!" he shouted. "Fire!"

James gathered up his mother

and raced outside.

Of course, the house wasn't on fire at all.

And James' mother was beside herself,

standing on the road in her nightclothes

for all the neighbors to see.

"James!" She stamped her foot.

"What is wrong with you!"

"But I smelled smoke," he said.
Then he sneezed three more times.
And finally he remembered the stranger,
who sneezed thrice before he disappeared.
"Could I be smelling," James wondered,
"into the future?"

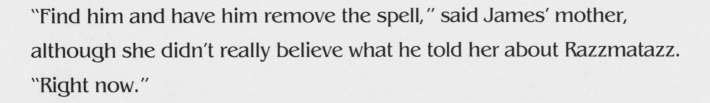

"Find him and have him remove the spell," said James' mother,
although she didn't really believe what he told her about Razzmatazz.
"Right now."

So James left the farm
in the dead of night
to look for the wizard.

After days of searching high and low
and far and wide, James arrived in the city.
A great banner was stretched high
over the main street:

24

ALL SOOTHSAYERS, FORTUNE-TELLERS, CRYSTAL-GAZERS,
WITCHES, AND WIZARDS ARE TO REPORT TO THE CASTLE.
BY ORDER OF THE KING.

He went straight to the castle.
"I'm looking for a wizard," he said,
"named Razzmatazz."

"No wizards have reported here,"
said a guard in charge of the gate,
"by that or any other name.
If only they had."

"What does the king want with wizards?" James asked.

"They can look into the future," said the other guard,
"and tell the king if his enemies
are coming by land or by sea."

"I may be able to help," James offered.
"I can smell into the future."

The guards shrugged—and why not?
But they showed James into the king's chambers.

"Smell into the future?" said the king doubtfully.
"How does that work?"

James had a hard time sneezing.

First he thought of a big bowl of ground pepper,

but nothing happened.

Then he thought of a great bag of feathers . . .

again, not even a wheeze.

Finally he thought of a closetful of cats,

and he sneezed three times:

"Hah-choo, -choo, -choo!"

"Well?" said the king.

James took a deep breath.

"What does the sea smell like?" he asked.

"Damp. And salty," the king replied.

James took another deep breath.

"Fishy?" he said.

The king nodded his head.

"That's it, then," said James.

"I'm sure of it. They're coming by sea."

So it came to pass.

The king turned back his enemies,

and James was feted and made much of.

The king wanted to reward him

by making him Court Sneezer for Life,

but James was homesick and tired of adventures.

30 His mother had sent a telegram:

"Fierce storm. Cows lost. House burned down. All is forgiven.

Love, Mother."

"But I would like one thing,"

James said to the king.

"What is that?" the king asked.

"A boat," said James, "with wheels."

James was taking no chances.

The wizard had told him he would spend

the rest of his life on a boat,

and so he did, right next to the barn.

James married and had three children,
all of whom knew what they would be eating
for dinner two weeks in advance.
The youngest became the best fire chief
in the country.